Daniel Fuller

The Diary of the Revd. Daniel Fuller

With His Account of His Family & Other Matters

Daniel Fuller

The Diary of the Revd. Daniel Fuller
With His Account of His Family & Other Matters

ISBN/EAN: 9783337033293

Printed in Europe, USA, Canada, Australia, Japan

Cover: Foto ©Raphael Reischuk / pixelio.de

More available books at **www.hansebooks.com**

The *DIARY* of the Rev^d

DANIEL FULLER

With his Account of His Family

& other matters. Written at *Gloucester*, in *Maſſachuſetts,* circa 1775, & edited by his Grandſon, DANIEL FULLER APPLETON.

One hundred copies imprinted for private diſtribution, at the DE VINNE PRESS, No. *12 Lafayette Place*, in the City of New-York. 1894.

THE REV. DANIEL FULLER, my maternal grandfather, lived between the years 1740 and 1829. He was graduated at Harvard College; was ordained a clergyman of the Congregational Church, January 10, 1770, having been called as associate pastor of the west parish of Gloucester, Massachusetts, in 1769. Becoming full pastor on the death of the Rev. Richard Jaques in 1777, he continued in this ministration — his only parish — for fifty years.

He was a typical country parson of the old school, "passing rich on forty pounds a year." (His salary was actually seventy pounds a year, and the use of the parsonage wood-lot; but during the War of the Revolution, and again during the second war with England, when by reason of distress and poverty his people were unable to meet their pecuniary obligations to him, he remitted this amount and encouraged his flock to bear the hardships incident to their struggle for liberty and their rights.)

His biography is given modestly and succinctly in his own words in the manuscript written for his children's information, "that they might not be ignorant of their lineage and descent," which is reprinted in these pages; and to his own words I do not see that I can add anything. His sons and daughters to the third and fourth generation have risen up to call him blessed, according to the scriptural promise, and his and their seed are like the sands of the sea on many shores. And his exact and conscientious methods, love of literal truth, his patriotism and exaltation in the self-sacrifice and achievements of his compatriots in the War of the Revolution, to whose patriot soldiery he contributed his ministrations as voluntary chaplain, are sufficiently displayed in the diary now reprinted from the original in my possession.

Upon their arriving at the age of fourteen years, he "bound" (after the custom of the day, and as he was himself bound) his male children to reputable artisans, that each might learn a useful trade, trusting to their own bents to lead them, as his own bent had led himself, to seek education and a learned profession, if so it pleased Providence. Although holding himself in line with the rigid tenets of his vocation, he was not wanting in that sense of humor which was often the amenity of the hard regimen of the Puritan pastor, and he used to tell of a poor man who came to him one spring to be married, offering, in payment for that service, to plant his potatoes! The service was rendered, and in the fall of the same year the man came back and offered to dig and harvest the potatoes if the parson would unmarry him. To which Mr. Fuller replied that the knot he had fixed in the spring was one "which you could tie with your tongue, but could not untie with your teeth!" He died at the house of his son Benjamin, in Dorchester, May 23, 1829. The meeting-house where he preached for half a century was, as appears from the picture of it here reproduced, a great barn-like structure, built, after the stern fashion of the day—foursquare and without the slightest amelioration of its lines,—of timbers rudely hewn from the inclosing forests. It has now entirely disappeared, but its site is the wildest and rockiest of spots to-day, and repels by the rugged barrenness of its desolation.

His youngest daughter, Sarah (born January 29, 1787; died January 7, 1872), married November 15, 1807, my father, James Appleton, then of Gloucester, afterward Brigadier-General of Massachusetts State Troops. Although a Federalist by connection and political preference, and so opposed to the policy which precipitated the second war with England, as soon as his country had committed itself to that war, General Appleton promptly volunteered his services in the field.

He served during that war as Lieutenant-Colonel of the Gloucester Regiment — certified as the Second Regiment, First Brigade, Second Division, of the Massachusetts Line. He twice, at the engagements of Sandy Bay and of Gallup's Folly, in 1814, repelled attacks of the British fleet under Sir George Colier upon the city and forts of Gloucester, for which services he was borne as of the same rank upon the rolls of the Regular Army of the United States. He subsequently was promoted Colonel, and Brigadier-General of the First Brigade, Second Division, of the Massachusetts Line, being honorably discharged as of that rank, June 15, 1827.

It will be seen that, in his chronological account, my grandfather finds his first ancestor in Thomas Fuller, the emigrant who, according to his own verses, came to New England in 1638 out of curiosity, intending

> . . . to ſtay one Year
> And here to ſtay no more.

This Mr. Thomas Fuller, however, stayed to some purpose, and has other claims to be remembered by his posterity than as a writer of verses. Among the earliest settlers of Middleton, he became one of its most considerable and wealthiest proprietors, and a large part of that town his descendants have occupied and improved to this day. Here he founded the second iron-working establishment in the present limits of the United States, iron having been discovered in the boggy soil thereabouts. And it is a singular fact, too, that the only earlier iron-works in the country were owned and operated in the neighboring town of Saugus, from ore taken from the same character of soil by Samuel Appleton, another ancestor of the Ipswich family into which the daughter of Daniel Fuller married. Among his descendants were many whose names have an interest other than local: Archelaus, a brother of the Rev. Daniel Fuller, the writer of the Diary, who was an aide-de-camp on General Washington's staff, and a member of the First, Second, and Third Continental Congresses. He died, at the early age of forty-five years, from disease contracted in the Quebec campaign. Of later date, the famous Margaret Fuller Ossoli was a descendant.

THE Diary here reprinted comes to me written in my grandfather's characteristically neat chirography, in a blank book of the size followed in this reprint, and bound in the familiar pigskin vellum of that date. This book he had used in his college days in studying trigonometry and the advanced problems of land-surveying, and in dividing and plotting in the now obsolete science of "Dialling," which was the art of constructing sun-dials. In this forgotten science the diagrams in the book before me are most elaborately and carefully drawn, and the rules for ascertaining the exact hour, not only by day but by night, are extremely intricate and interesting, and set down in very careful penmanship.

This exercise-book survived college days, and Mr. Fuller utilized its blank pages thereafter as a commonplace book, in which to note points for his sermons, historical items of passing or permanent interest to him, matters to him of unusual reference, etc., together with such memoranda of political records of his day, and of the then growing Federal commonwealth, as the following:

> The President chosen 4th of December but his presidency is not entered up untill ye 4th of March. The election is to be once in four years. Mr. Thomas Jefferson chosen President of the United States of America by Ballot 1803. The judges are appointed by ye Confederate Congress.

Here also are the laboriously copied accounts of a trial for witchcraft, of a case of religious frenzy (or, as he labels it, "an Enthusiasm") in South Carolina, and the like, and many reflections of his own as to "Affectation," "Profanity," "Dress," etc., etc.

Upon such blank pages, or portions of pages, as still

remained, Mr. Fuller commences, in the momentous days of 1775, to note the stirring and stormy events which began to transpire and thicken about him. Most interesting of all are the simple entries of events then incidental, but since of such momentous importance — the item:

April 19, 1775. This day we were alarmed Upon ye defcent of a Party of Regulars leaving Bofton very early, when arived at Lexington they killed Several Perfens and did other Mifchief.

and, in immediate juxtaposition, the following:

The Widow Stevens with her daughter, Son Samuel & wife moved to my houfe.

That was the shot fired by the "embattled farmers" "heard round the world."

Again:

June 17th, 1775. The Provincials & Regular Troops from Bofton had a very fmart engagement at Bunkers Hill Charleftown.

So quietly did my ancestor note a day and an event upon which, in the glowing diction of Daniel Webster, "all subsequent history has poured its light."

Here, too, are the notes of his itineraries taken as voluntary chaplain among the patriot soldiers gathered about Charlestown and Boston, faithfully and often fantastically grouped with domestic and pastoral details, New Year and family calls and visitations, and the like.

Of course the items relating to the war in precincts remote from his own environment were written in later, and partook of the old purpose of the common-place book. But the dates are always, as was the writer's wont, as exact and brief as are those within his personal knowledge, his dislike for anything savoring of exaggeration or possible misinformation being curiously indicated in one or two instances, where, having set down the valuation of a prize captured by the Gloucester privateers (who rendered such inestimable services to the patriot quartermasters) at a given figure, he carefully erased that figure, and left the entry blank, on a later suspicion, perhaps, of their too generous proportions.

While these entries are, of course, of concern only to Mr. Fuller's descendants, they are of wider interest at least in showing everywhere the pride with which he himself and his contemporaries regarded the achievements of the yeoman soldiery and sailors, and the fervent confidence which all about him felt in the ultimate success of the patriot cause. In this, at any rate, this Diary — kept in times when, as is a very conspicuous matter of fact, personal diaries were few and far between, and men were men of deeds rather than scribes—is certainly some small contribution to our actual history.

Mr. Fuller's entries, it will be seen, are most frequent in the years 1775 and 1776. Perhaps the crowding events of subsequent years precluded much attention to personal records. The first and last items, as will be seen, are personal. But for the members of his family the Diary is of sufficient interest, I think, to warrant this effort for its preservation.

I desire to add my acknowledgments to my nephew, Appleton Morgan, Esq., of New York City, a great-grandson of the Rev. Mr. Fuller, for his assistance in preparing the Diary for the printer.

DANIEL FULLER APPLETON.

IPSWICH, MASSACHUSETTS,
July 1, 1894.

A Chronological Account of the Family and Defcendants of Thomas Fuller.

A Chronological Account of the Family and Defcendants of Thomas Fuller.

IT is very unaccountable that there are fo many of the firft fettlers of this country who have been fo defficient in giving us thier defcendants an Account of thier family, the Place of thier Nativity, the Place of thier Firft Settlement here, and the occafion of their emigration &c in writing; when, at the fame Time it does appear from Tradition, in fome Cafes, that they were not unacquainted with Letters and the Art of Writing.

It appears from Tradition, that my great grandfather by My Father's fide, Thomas Fuller & great great-grandfather by my mother's fide had fomewhat of a Poetical Turn of Mind: for I have collected a Few Verfes from Aged People, faid to be his compofition, that he was urged to allow them to be carried to the Prefs, but the matter was never accomplifhed.

That you, my dear Children, might not be altogether Ignorant of your lineage and Defcent from this common ftock, of the Defign of his coming to New England

land (which feems to have been out of curiofity, for he defigned to have tarried but one year,) the occafion of his tarrying here (which was, it alfo feems, on account of Religion) And of the Bleffings that have followed his Offfpring to the fourth and fifth generation, for I have never known or heard that any of his feed have been put to the hard Neceffity of begging thier Bread. On this Account, I have been at the pains of collecting and now commit to writing the following chronological Account.

In the year 1620, in ye month of December the Plymouth Company arrived at old Plymouth in New England. And about eighteen years after—in 1638—Thomas Fuller came to a place then called Salem Village, now called Middleton—1638. There he purchafed a Tract of wild land, built a Houfe near a Streem about half a mile below Middleton Pond fouth of Wilts Hill. His houfe was near the fpot where the Revd Mr. Smith now lives. He had fix fons and one Daughter, Thomas, John, Jacob, Benjamin, Jofeph, Samuel, and Ruth.—Thomas 2nd had fix fons Thomas, Jonathan, John, Jofeph, William and Stephen. No Daughters. John the firft no Sons, two Daughters. Jacob Second, two fons. Edward and Jacob, and three daughters, Mary, Betty and Sarah. Benjamin 1st two fons Samuel (married a Bacon, December 15th 1685) and Benjamin, and four Daughters Sarah, Ruth, Abigail and Hannah. Jofeph the

firft

firſt and Samuel the firſt, were not married. Ruth 1ſt married a Wheeler. She left only one Daughter, Ruth. Thomas 3rd, married a Baxton, (and had) three sons John, Joſeph and Timothy, four Daughters, Elizabeth, Ruth, Mary and Lydia. Samuel 2nd (had) three ſons, James, Joſhua and Samuel, and three Daughters, Mary, Miriam and Abigail. (Theſe are my Father's Brother's children.) Benjamin 2nd married Mary Fuller — (Thos 3rds daughter) (and had) ſix ſons, Archelaus, Daniel 1ſt, Andrew 1ſt, Elijah theſe three laſt died young 2nd Daniel 2nd Andrew. Two Daughters Sarah died when ſhe was about thirteen years old, and one child ſtill born. Archelaus 1ſt (had) three ſons, Elijah, Benjamin, Daniel. Elijah died a little after he was out of his time. Five Daughters. Sarah and Hannah, by his firſt wife. Hannah, Richardſon, Betty, Sarah and Mary, Benjamin and Daniel by his ſecond wife, Betty Putnam, widow (maiden name Dale). Hannah married Joſeph Hutchinſon. They had four ſons Elijah, Joſeph, Archelaus and Levi. Betty Putnam (had) two daughters Betty and Lucy. Sarah Putnam had two daughters, Sarah and Elizabeth, and three ſons, Iſrael, Fuller, and Samuel.

Daniel (myſelf), born September 1ſt, 1740. At about fourteen years of age I was put an apprentice to Joſeph Fuller of Middleton, carpenter and ſhipjoiner. At about ſeventeen began to learn Latin. At twenty, about

about the year 1760, I entered Cambridge College, and took my firſt degree in 1764. The ſpring before, myſelf and brother Andrew took the ſmallpox by enoculation at Charleſtown. I kept ſchool at Old Hampton, New Hampſhire, 1765, and at Haverhill, Maſſachuſetts, 1767. Removed to my Fathers, ſtudied Divinity, and took my ſecond Degree 1766. Began to preach 1768. Came to preach at Cape Ann July 1769. Was ordained colledge paſtor with the Revd Richard Jaques, ſecond church Glouceſter, January 10th 1770. Auguſt 14th was married to Hannah Bowers, born September 17, 1750 the daughter of the Revd Benjamin Bowers of Middleton, Conneticut. December 1750 began to keep Houſe at Cape Ann. Houſe formerly Rev. Mr. Jaques's. Aug. 27th 1771 our eldeſt daughter Hannah Peters, was born. Aug. 27, 1773 Daniel was born. February 27, 1776, Benjamin was born. April 1, 1770 Elijah was born. September 11, 1780 Archelaus was born. October 22nd 1782 Samuel Newell was born. February 18, 1785, Mary was born. June 27th 1787, Sarah, was born. My son Daniel at about the age of fourteen years went to live with Capt. David Hinkley at New Braintry, returned home Auguſt, 1793. Benjamin at about the age of fifteen years was Bound to John Mycall of Newberry to learn the art of Printing. Elijah at about the age of fourteen years went to live with Mr. Joſeph Wood, Cape Ann Harbor, to learn the Tin Man's Trade.

Trade. Archelaus at about the age of ſixteen years went to Newberry port to learn the art of Portrait Painting &c of Mr. Benjamin Tucker. Samuel at about the age of fourteen went to Bridgton near Port Land to live with his brother Daniel in trade. Benjamin, January 1st 1798 Hired a ſtore in Boſton, near to Boſton Stone. He was married to Marcia Beal of Boſton, July 13th 1800.

MIDDLE HADDAM, CONNECTICUT, NEW ENGLAND.

Revd Benjamin Bowers was born March 7, 1713–14.

Sarah Newhall, his wife, was born January 17th 1718–19.

Their Children

1 Benjn born July 16, 1743
2 Sarah " Aug 1st 1745
3 Hannah, born June 2nd 1745
4 Jonathan, born May 19, 1749
Died Oct. 17th 1749
5 Hannah Born Sept 1750
6 Mary born Oct 16th 1752
7 Jonathan born Oct 15th 1754
8 Lydia born July 11, 1756

Mrs Bowers departed this life July 31, 1757, 5 o'clock p m.

Sarah departed this life Oct 26—1766.

The Revd Benjamin Bowers departed this life May 10, 1761.

The Meditations and Experiences of Thos Fuller of Salem Village, Now Called Middleton, with his Advice to his Children in Verſe (1638)

The

The Meditations and Experiences of Thos Fuller of Salem Village, Now· Called Middleton, with his Advice to his Children in Verſe (1638)

I

In thirty eight I ſet my foot
Upon New England's ſhore
My thoughts were then to ſtay one Year
And here to ſtay no more.

II

But by the preaching of God's word
By famous Shepherd. He
In what a woful ſtate I was
I then began to ſee.

III

My father was an Amorite
And I am Hittite born
In all the blood of filthyness
I ſaw myſelf ſolorn.

IV Chriſt

IV

Chrift caft his Garments over me
And all my Sins did cover
More precious to my Soul was he
Than deareft Friend or Lover.

V

His pardoning mercy to my Soul
All thoughts did far furmount
The Bowells of his Love to me
Was quite beyond account.

VI

Sometimes I am upon the Hill
And I fee the City clear
I knew twas New Jerufalem
I was to it fo near.

VII

I faid thy Mountain does ftand firm
And doubtlefs t'will forever
But when God turned his face away
This Joy from me did fever.

VIII

A Mary Magdalen, of whom
The Scriptures do us tell

That

That ſeven Devils & no leſs
At once in her did dwell.

IX

Manaſſah, too, whoſe ſins did all
Vile Ephrahims ſar exceed
In that he cauſ'd Jeruſalem
Moſt cruelly to bleed.

X

But oh God's mercy how timely
It comes, to each of theſe
Chriſt's Precious Blood ſufficient was
God's Anger to Appeaſe!

XI

Sure Ephraim is a pleaſant Child,
A ſon to me moſt dear
And ſince againſt him I have ſpoke
My Bowells troubled are.

XII

Sometimes I am in mountains High,
Sometimes in Vallies low
The ſtate that Man's in here below
Does oft times ebb and flow.

XIII

I heard the Voice of God, by Man
Yet Sorrows held me faſt
But theſe my Joys did far exceed
God heard my voice at laſt.

XIV

Satan flung fiery darts at me
And thought the day to win
Becauſe he knew he had a Friend
That always dwelt within.

XV

But ſurely God will ſave my ſoul
And though you Trouble have
My Children Dear, who fear the Lord
Your Souls at Death Will Save.

XVI

All Tears ſhall then be wipt away
And Joys beyond Compare,
Where Jeſus is and Angells dwell
With every Saint you'll Share.

Finis.

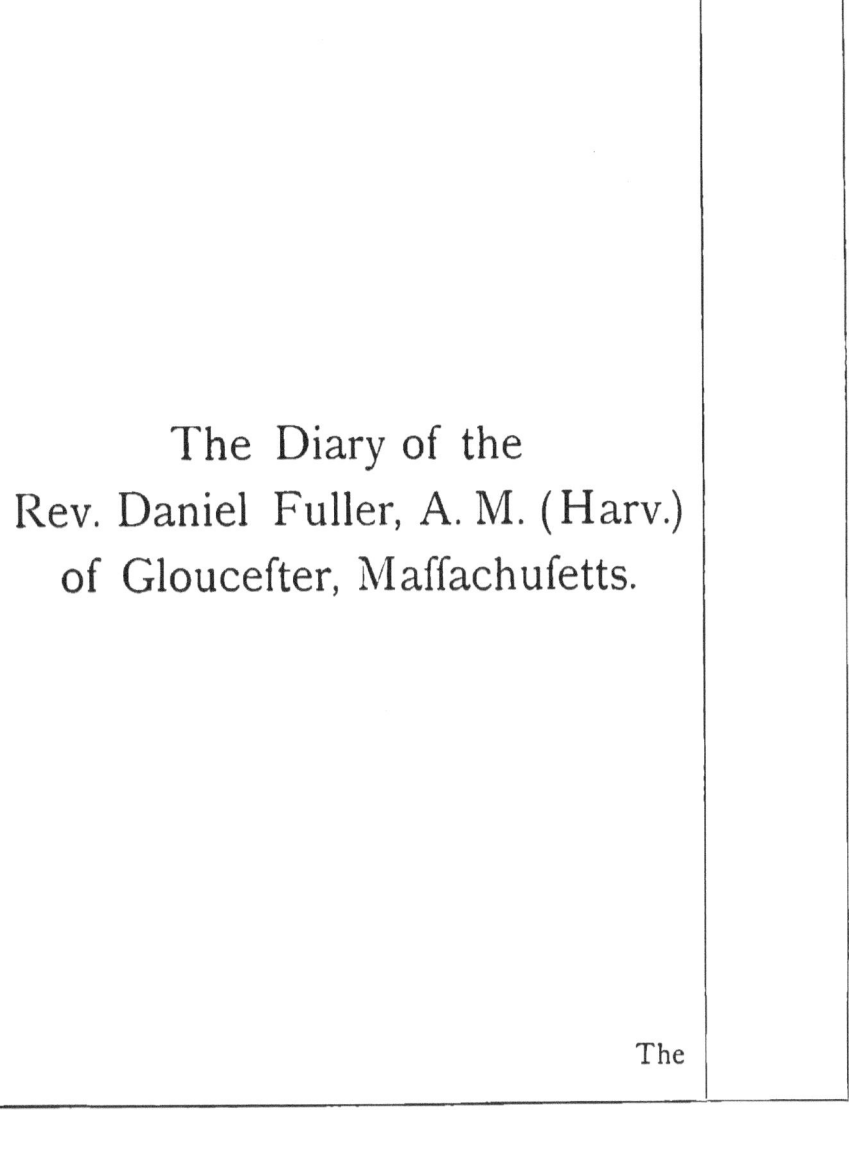

The Diary of the Rev. Daniel Fuller, A. M. (Harv.) of Gloucefter, Maffachufetts.

The

The Diary of the Rev. Daniel Fuller, A. M. (Harv.) of Gloucester, Massachusetts.

1775.

THE first of this month I & my wife went to Middleton to attend the Funeral solemnities of My Dear Father. We arrived safely at my Mother's. How are all things changed? A Mother overwhelmed with grief, saying, this is Trouble such as I never met with before. A solemn meeting of Brothers. Sorrow stops ye course of utterance. And a Pause ensues! That Hand & that Tongue which welcomed Children to a Father's house, by Reason of Death are now silent and cold! O cruel Death! what very Friends and Lovers hast thou separated? equally regardless of ye Widows Tears. & ye Cryes of the Fatherless. *March 1, 1775.*

" How vain are all things here below
" How false and yet how fair
" Each Pleasure has its Poison too
" Every sweet a Snare

" The

"The brighteſt things below ye ſky
"Give but a flattering light
"We ſhould expect ſome Danger nigh
"When we Poſſeſs Delight."

After Paying our laſt ſolemn Rites to our dear father's Remains we returned, and thro' ye Goodneſs of God to uſward find our family well — May not ye voice of ye Dead be preſently forgot, ſaying to us be ye alſo Ready.

About this time made an exchange with the Revd Mr. Cutler,[1] cold and uncomfortable Weather for ye Seaſon. Toward ye latter End of this month two ſnow ſtorms.

March 16, 1775. The Revd Mr. Chandler Departed this Life (who was 14 years miniſter of ye Firſt Chr. in Glouceſter) in ye 85 year of his age.

March 22, 1775. About this Time preached for ye Revd Mr. Tappan Newbery.

March 24, 1775. The Britiſh Troopes Evacuated Boſton, New England. Six thouſand in number — Experienced Warriors for Nova Scotia.

This

[1] Manasseh Cutler, of the Hamlets, now Hamilton, Member of Congress, author of the Ordinance of 1787, and promoter of first settlement of Ohio.

This day we were alarmed Upon y[e] defcent of a Party of Regulars leaving Bofton very early, when arived at Lexington they killed Several Perfens and did other Mifchief. *April* 19, 1775.

The Widow Stevens with her daughter, Son Samuel & wife moved to my houfe. *April* 21, 1775.

People in this Parifh chiefly employed in removing Houfe Hold Furniture and Provifion of all kinds from y[e] Harbours to this Place. Preached, but very few people attended, the flight was on the Sabbath. The Horrid Maffacre committed by the fore mentioned Regulars under the command of Col. Smith greatly alarmed us. Never faw fuch a Sabbath before. The ever to be dreaded Sword of Civil War is drawn. The Lord grant y[t] it may be fpeedily fheathed again. *April* 23, 1775.

Mr. Jofiah Quincy arrived at our Harbor from England and Soon after died on bord the fhip. The guns at Penopfhut fort taken away by General Gage's Order.

The Harbour Chh and Parifh in order to Refettle a Gofpel Minifter—kept this day as a Day of Fafting and Prayer. Prefent the Rev[d] Mr Roggers of Town, who preached A. M. The Rev[d] Mr Cleaveland who made the Firft Prayer. P. M. and myfelf Clofed with Prayer. *April* 26, 1775.

April 28, 1775. I and my wife Dined at Col^l. Peter Coffins in company with the Revd Eli Forbes & Wife, the Revd Obadiah Parſons & wife. The above ſaid Mr. Quincey was interred at the Harbour Pariſh. He had been to England on publick Buſineſs, had ſeveral Conferences with Lord North and Dartmouth — much was expected from ſo Ingenious and intelligent a Man. But we are deprived of it,— a great power of Providence at ſuch a critical Time.

May 1, 1775. Hired a man to ſet ſome Grafts, tranſplanted ſome Mulberry and Apple trees.

May 2, 1775. Walked to Chebacco to attend the Revd John Cleavelands Quarterly Faſt. Miniſter's Preſent the Revd Eli Forbes — the Revd Eben Cleaveland. The Revd Obidiah Parſons & my ſelf.

May 3, 1775. The Revd Eli Forbes & Lady & Col. Coffin's Lady were at my Houſe.

May 7, 1775. Sowed Some Hay Seed. We are Credibly informed that the People of New York and New Jerſey have taken New York Fort from the Poſſeſſion of the King's troops, and have Prevented General Gage's veſſels from importing any thing from thence.

May 7, 1775. Sacrament day.

Went

A View of the Old Church at West Parish, C[illegible] Mass.
built 1714.

May 8, 1775.

Went to ſee Mr. Urion Stevens ſick of a Feaver. Stoped at John Haſkell's Widow's, two Families in her Chamber one of the Children an Infant very ill.

Viſited at Arion Haſkells at David Haſkell's & at the Revd Mr. Jaques's & Sons. Their youngeſt Daughter Dangerouſly ill.

Continental Congreſs is to meet at Philadelphia. The Provincial Congreſs have agreed to have a Standing army ſtationed at Cambridge to conſiſt of 30000 men. Connecticut ſends 6000 Rodiland 1500.

May 11, 1775.

A day of humbleſt faſting and prayer over the Province.

May 12, 1775.

Had my garden Plowed and dug by Caleb Lufkin. The General Aſſembly of Connecticut have Reſolved yt an Embargo be placed upon the exportation by Water of Wheat, Rye, Indian Corn, Pork, Beef, Live Cattle, Peas, Beans, Bread, Flower, & every kind of Meal to continue to 20 of May. Senators of the Congreſs of America are appointed by the individual States.

May 13, 1775.

Rev Eben Cleaveland at my Houſe. Exchanged with him.

May 15, 1775.

Hannah Peters went to School — Revd Mr Parſons & wife & Daughter at my houſe. Times very diſ-treſſing, more Troops arrived, & more expected.

Trees

May 16, 1775.	Trees full in their Bloſſom. Proſpect of a Fruitful year. Planting & Sowing my garden.
May 29, 1775.	Rode to Middleton in Company with Iſrael Eveleth, met an Alarm upon Cheboſſet Cauſeway, it was ſaid a Body of Regular Troops were landed & landing at Weſt Beach Beverley. It proved was Falſe. Dined at the Revd Mr Willard's, ſlept at My Mother's.
May 30, 1775.	Rode to Water-Town. Revd Dr Langdon Preached an election Sermon. Rode to Weſtown ſlept at ye Widow Gibbs with ye Revd Mr Wadſworth.
June 3, 1775.	The Revd Mr Stevens, of Kittery Preached at Watertown to the Convention of Miniſters we agreed to preach as Chaplins by Rotation thro' the Province to ye Provincial Army at Cambridge. Rode to Cambridge. Dined at Major Ezra Putnam's. Stroled a little about Town. The Troops have made Barracks of ye Colleges. Stoughton Southweſt Corner Second Story this Chamber converted into a Printing office. The ſoldiers in High Spirits, ſickly among ym. Attended ye Funeral of one of ym. Rhode down to ye Stone Houſe, ſaw ſome Indians belonging to ye Camp, doleful appearance y made indeed! Viewed ye Fortifications. Returned to Middleton. The Latter End of laſt week & ye Beginning of this Colonel Putnam with a Small Detachment brought from

from Hog & Noddles' Iſlands Five Hundred Sheep, a Number of Cows & Horſes, & Since that more from Dear Iſland a little below, burnt an armed ſchooner, took a ſmall boat with three or four men in Her. Set Boat & Men in ye Boat into a Waggon drove to Cambridge all this without ye loſs of a Man.

Two tranſports lay off in Ipſwich bay. *June* 4, 1775.

Viſited at Mr Bynton's. *June* 10, 1775.

Exchanged with Mr Toppan of Mancheſter at Marble Head Harbor a few Men retake a veſſel loaded with Molaſſes & other Weſtindia goods from a Man of War in ye Night which the Man of War Men did not diſcover until ſome Time Next Day. *June* 11, 1775.

We are credibly informed y^{t} at Noodle's Iſland two Provincials being ſort with Cannon from a Man of War, they ventured ſo near as to return ye Fire with thier muſkets, it is ſaid killed a Man upon ye Shrouds took up ſome of thier Shott and walked off unhurt.

Went to Beverly to ſetch the News Papers. Met Cap^{n} Collins's Company in the way to Cambridge, And a Number of Harbour Gentle Men at Mancheſter at Dea^{n} Allens Tavern — we Rode up in Marſhall order, Major Rogge led the Van, & Major Whittemore brought up the Rear. *June* 15, 1775.

Our

June 16, 1775.	Our Troops began an Intrenchment on Bunkers Hill Charlestown.
June 17, 1775.	The Provincials & Regular Troops from Boston had a very smart engagement at Bunkers Hill Charlestown — Charlestown at ye Same Time supposed to contain about 300 dwelling houses besides 150 or 200 other buildings were almost all laid in ashes by General Gage's Order.
July 5, 1775.	My Horse Kicked one of my Leggs, by which I was very Lame.
July 6, 1775.	Rode in my Chaise to Col Coffin's.
July 7, 1775.	Invited to dine at Zebulon Haskell's . . . Mr William Ellery at Table—Rev^{d} Mr Forbes at my House.
July 9, 1775.	Sabbath, not able to Preach, by Reason of my Lameness.
July 16, 1775.	Sabbath, my Leg very Lame. Not able to preach.
July 18, 1775.	Election of Councillors in This Province.
July 19, 1775.	Fast Day — The Continental Congress. North American Recommended a General Fast to be on this Day & we learn y^{t} Twelve of our Provinces Professed Religiously to keep the same — Preached on Said Day. Mr.

Mr. Appleton[1] of Ipſwich preached for me. *July* 23, 1775.

Alarmed in this Pariſh. Capt. Linſey lay off Squam river. Sent a barge with fifty men who attempted to Land on Col. Coffin's Beach; but were Repulſed by a briſk firing of our People. Faſt days are on Thurſdays. *August* 5, 1775.

Sacrament Day. *August* 6, 1775.

I, my wife and oldeſt child Hannah Peters rode to Middleton. Found my mother & kindred well. *August* 7, 1775.

I & my wife rode to Wobourn Precinct. Dr Win, all well Molley lately recovered from the Small Pox. We rode in company with Molley Win to Roxſbury, ſtopped at ye Sine of Ye Punch Bowl. There Saw Father Boardman Chaplin. I rode to ye top of Roxſbury Hill, found Brother Jonathan Bowers in ye Service. Slep at Jamaica Plains, I was at Revd Mr Gorden's. *August* 7, 1775.

Lyndſey, capt of a man of war, fired it is ſuppoſed near 300 Shot at ye Harbour Pariſh. Damaged ye meeting Houſe ſomewhat, & ſome other Buildings. Not a Single Perſon killed or wounded with his Cannon Shott. We Retook two veſſels belonging to Salem, his barge & another Boat, alſo we took together with ym *August* 8, 1775.

[1] This was the Rev. Joseph Appleton, father of the late William Appleton, merchant, of Boston; afterward Minister of Brookfield, Massachusetts.

y^m about thirty of thier men, with the lofs of only two of our Men. His Boatfwain likewife in attempting to fet the town on fire by Firing the Train of Powder to fome combuftable Matter prepared, providentially the fire was communicated to ye powder iron in his hand which occafioned an explofion and it is faid he loft his Hand if not his Life.

August 10, 1775. Returned to Col. Spencer's Lodging, took our Leave of Father Boardman & Brother Bowers. Dined at Captn Eveleth's Tent. Profpect Hill. By Reafon of ye Rain which fell in great plenty, were prevented from viewing ye intrenchments upon ye Summit of f^d Hill. Returned to Woobourn, flept at Dr Win's.

August 11, 1775. After dinner fett off for Middleton—drank a Glafs of Wine at ye Rev. Mr Haven's Reading. Slept at my Mother's.

August 12, 1775. Rev^d Mr. Wadfworths, Danverfe, who engaged to preach by way of exchange for me the next Sabbath.

August 13, 1775. Preached for the Rev. Mr. French, Andover, who preached at Beverley, for the Rev. Mr. Hitchcock at Danverfe.

August 15, 1775. The Rev^d Mr. Smith's Youngeft Child died. Non-exportation takes place.

August 16, 1775. We returned to our Houfe, found all well. Bleffed be be ye Name of Our God for His Goodnefs to me & Mine, may it lead us to unfained Repentance & engage us to Walk with Him all ye Days of our Lives!

An Armed Schooner brought into our Harbor, a Ship taken by a Man of War from Portfmouth bound to Weft Indies which it retook. *September* 7, 1775.

Brother and crew came to my Houfe. Left his Family & our Friend. *September* 9, 1775.

He kept Sabbath with me. *September* 10, 1775.

We rode to ye Harbor in ye Morning. In ye afternoon to Danverfe. *September* 11, 1775.

Went to Middleton, Brother Archalaus & oldeft Son fick of Fevers. After Noon returned to my family & found y^{m} thro ye goodnefs of God in ufual health, overtook fome Rifle men on ye march to retake Quebec & the other Weftern forts now in Poffeffion of ye King's Troops. *September* 12, 1775.

The Rev^{d} Mr. Williams of Newcafco came to my houfe, lodged with me. *September* 14, 1775.

Rode to Captain Norwoods & dined there with ye Rev^{d} Mr. Williams & Parfons of Squam. Then Rode to Mr. Clevelands Parifh. Lodged at Dr. Pools. *September* 16, 1775.

October 3, 1775. A Diploma was given admitting a Number of Gentlemen to y^{r} Firſt & Second Degree — About this time a large quantity of wood came into Squam River occaſioned by a Freſhet in Marimac River it is ſaid enough to ſupply the Pariſh of Squam thro the Winter.

October 19, 1775. The Canieaux — Capt Mowat, with four other armed Veſſels, came From Boſton to Caſco Bay.

October 20, 1775. They ſet ye town on Fire. Without any oppoſition they attempted to ſet ye meeting houſe on Fire but did not ſucceed.

October 30, 1775. A Company of Five & Thirty came From Ipſwich to this Town to aſſiſt in ſortifying our Harbour.

October 31, 1775. We had a general Muſter in order to view Arms.

November 3, 1775. The fort St Johns near Montreal. This Garriſon Surrendered this Day, to General Montgomery.

November 27, 1775. An Oiſter Boat Retaken by Cap Bradbury Saunders, in our harbour.

November 28, 1775. The Privateer Capt Manley Maſter brought into our Harbour Capann a Brig laden with military ſtores valued at Thirty Thouſand pounds ſterling. N. B. Had on Board a Fine Braſs morter weight ^{ll} 27 ^{qa} 2.

&

& fome odd Pounds, at the fame Time brought in a Sloop in ye Service of ye Minifterial troops.

December 3, 1775.

The aforefaid Privateer carried into Beverly a Ship laden with Sea Coal, Rum, Wine Clothing &C &C valued at 30.000.[1]

December 12, 1775.

Rode to Middleton, found my Friends in Health. Poor Elijah died laft Month. The Deareft Friends and Relatives muft Part. May we have a happy meeting in ye Wd of Glory.

December 13, 1775.

Rode to Medford. And walk'd from thence to Winter Hill. Slept at Col. Hutchinfons Barracks. Saw Major Ezra Putnam fick with the jaundice.

December 14, 1775.

Took a walk in the morning amongft the Barracks upon Winter Hill. How does the effects of Horrid War alter ye appearance of Things! Where are thofe beautiful Walks and valuable Nurferies of —— that once adorned this Spot! Cut off unfinifhed by a moft unnatural war. O cruel Mother Country if you may be fo called, come take a walk with me. Look around. Behold ye Hardy, ye Valliant fons of Freedom. Intrepid Warriors, tho not bred to Arms yet not in ye manual Servife unfkilled. See the effect of a few months!

[1] This valuation appears to have been subsequently erased by Mr. Fuller.

months! Commodious Barracks. Impregnable Fortreſſes. Mark yon Summit the Hights of Charleſ-Town, there Bled—To your Diſhonor and Diſgrace it muſt be ſaid! many, many of ye Flower of Your Troops. View ye Ruins at ye Foot of ye Hill upon ye Right Hand, of yr once Flouriſhing Town, laid in aſhes by a Tyrant's Command. Stretch your View further to Boſton. Think how its Inhabitants ye Sons of Freedom have deſerted thier pleaſant Habitations or profitable honeſt Imployments becauſe of your cruel Inhumane Treatment! See your half Famiſhed Troops beſeaging but ſtrange to relate — beſeaged — thier Tirant Maſters and Cruel Mother.

Ploughed-Hill near Charleſton Common. This fort is well conſtructed, we erected it in the mouth of your cannon, and Still Hold with undaunted Courage. Cobble Hill, ſouthweſt of Bunkers Hill, no opposition tho' you ſee your water caſtle or man of war lyes hard by. See there ſouthward our Buſy Soldiery have built a Bridge & are completing a cauſeway in order to erect a fort upon yonder point of land Leachmores Point. Proſpect Hill. How well prepared we are. You Now may ſee to defend ourſelves & meet our Enemy. But you muſt be going. Take Head, beware, you ſtand upon Slippery ground adieu.

I returned to Middleton — gave at Medford my horſe one night my horſe 18S 9d.

Returned

Returned to Gloucefter. Capt Manly brought a prize into Beaverly—a floop loaded with Corn & Oates. *December 16, 1775.*

Our Privateers brought a Sloop into our Harbour laden with wood defigned for the befieged minifterial Troops in Bofton. *December 19, 1775.*

Four Quaker gentlemen came from the Southward to this Place to relieve the Poor. *December 20. 1775.*

1776.

The Year Begins with the continuance of an unhappy Civil War amongft us. *January 1, 1776.*

I went to ye Cove. Vifited at Mr. Chriftopher Hogg'shoufe & Mr. Bailey's, at Mr. William Morgain's & Mr. Andrews', at Mr. William Fords, & Mr. Andrews, at Mr. Trafk's, at Mr. Camble's—at Mr. Ruffell's—at Mr. Hibberts, at Captain Gilberts—at Mr. Jonathan Girberts' & walked home in ye Evening. Very cold and Slippery.

Preached a New Year's sermon. *January 14, 1776.*

Vifited at Mr. William Allins, at Ifaac Allins, at Saml Hadlocks, at Captn Blakes, at Captn Coofe's—at the Widow Stevens's, at Mr. Benj. Bifhop's, at Mrs. Ann Hafkell's, his daughter Nemone fick of a Confumption. *January 15, 1776.*

fumption. it Rained. very bad walking. A fhip from London & a Brig from Cork taken & carried to Newberry.

January 16, 1776. Went to David Hafkell's again, Daughter remains very ill. Vifited at Mr. Daniel Hafkells. The Revd Mr. Forbes's Wife at ye Harbor died about 9 oclock P. M.

January 17, 1776. Walked to ye Harbor by ye way of ye Ferry, ftopped at the Revd Mr. Boggerfes, dined at Major Lows, on my return vifited at Mr Ebeneezer Brays. Returned home, a very bad fnow ftorm.

March 7, 1776. The Britifh Troops precipitately Left ye Town of Bofton. The Virtue of Common Stinging Nettles, it is one of the moft efficient medicenes we have in the Vegitable Kingdom, in the form of a ftrong dicoction or Infufion, taken in the Quantity of a Pint in a Day it is a moft valuable Strengthener of a general or Particular Relaxation. In that of a weak Infufion, it proves a valuable alternative or Decobftruction of the Veffels, and in that of expreffed Juices, taken by Spoonfulls as ye exigency of ye cafe requires, it is the moft powerful Stiptich in internal Bleedings known. Externally applied as fermentation or Poultice it amazingly dyfpenfes or fcatters Inflamations & refolves Swellings. In the common fore throat, thus applied and internally in a gargle great dependence may fafely be put in this common plant.

One

One of ye Continental Frigates of 24 guns built at Newbury-Port under ye Direction of ye Hon. Thomas Cufhing Efq^{r} was launched. *May* 3, 1776.

Jofeph Coward came to my Houfe to Stay with me. *May* 6, 1776.

A continental Frigate of 32 guns, built at Portf-mouth under ye Direction of John Langdon Efq was launched, ye whole time from her raifing to ye Day of her launching did not exceed fixty working Days & was completely at her Anchors in ye main channel in lefs than Six months from ye time fhe run without ye leaft hurt. *May* 4, 1776.

Second Continental Faft. *May* 17, 1776.

Ruth Bray Came to my Houfe to tarry a little while. *June* 28, 1776.

Independence of the United States declared. *July* 4, 1776.

Battle at Trenton New Jerfey. *December* 26, 1776.

Preached here. Dined at Mr. Baker's, quiete a fickly time with y^{m}. Stopt at Col. Coffin's, faw ye Rev^{d} Mr. Forbes & wife. Returned from Brookfields. About this time a Brig from Canida, bound to Bofton with live ftock and other Neceffaries for the minifterial troops taken by the people of this town. *September* 17, 1776.

1777. Battle

1777.

August 16, 1777. Battle of Bennington which Preceeded General Burgoynes furrender of ye Britifh Army to General Gates.

1778.

January 9, 1778. I fent fifty dollars to him[1] by Mr. Jonathan Lord.[2]

February 6, 1778. A treaty of Friendfhip and Commerce Between ye United States and the court of Verfailles Was Signed y^s day.

1779.

July 5, 1779. An Army confifting of 2600 Troops Commander Governor Tryon landed at New Haven, Connec^t, where they wantonly did confiderable Damage. The feventh—deftroy the Town of Fairfield, burnt the Meeting Houfe—Done by the Refugee-Tories—The tenth they deftroyed Norwalk & Greenfield. Evergreen plants in ye Bloffom 10 of this month Manchefter—the Bafs woodtree Sweet agermony, a monthly Plant. Dea^n Rokets pafture, in ye Bloffom.

1780. Was

[1] Mr. Fuller's son Daniel.

[2] This entry was subsequently canceled on payment of the loan.

1780.

Was interred ye Wife of The Revd Eli Forbes, who departed this Life ye 6. Pall Holders ye Rev. John Rogers, John Cleaveland, Benj^a Tappan, Joseph Dana, Manassah Culler, Danl Fuller. *June* 9, 1780.

About 12 oclock A. M. came on an uncommon Darkness, some time previous to it the Clouds arose about South West remarkably black which Soon overspread ye Horizon. The Darkness increased to ye degree t^t we were obliged to light a Candle to dine by. This darkness continued till towards ye Sun going down. The Moon fulled ye 15th, yet it was so dark about Nine P. M. that in a Room where there were three large windows no glimpse of light could be Perceived no more y^n in a Dark Cellar. *May* 19, 1780.

Gloucester 2 Chu, the first time ye sacrament administered this year. *May* 20, 1780.

1781.

The Reduction of ye British Army under the Command of Lord Cornwallis at York, Gloucester, Virginia —General Washington, commander in chief of the Confederate army in America. *November* 19 1781.

A

November 25, 1781. A Man of War & a Tranfport Burnt by Lightning in our Bay.

November 26, 1781. A Sloop taken by the Privateers and brought into our Harbour loaded with Fifh & Train Oil. A violent Storm of fnow.

1783.

April 29, 1783. I rode to Ipfwich to attend upon the celebration of the American Peace, Mr John Cleaveland read the Proclamation in Mr Frifby's Meeting Houfe & Prayed. A Pfalm was Sung, After which thre Cannon were fired thirteen Times. The United States and French Flags were flying. Then all the Affembled People were Invited to dine. Tables fpread upon the Common. Then 13 Toafts were drank and Cannon Fired. Fire Works & Illumination were difplayed at Evening— Drank Tea at Dr Mannings and returned.

1784.

November 17, 1784. Had a Suit of Clothes made—Broad Cloth not fuperfine coft 1290 Dollars, making exclufive of trimmings 490 — 1790 Dollars.

1788. Bought

1788.

Bought for Dan[l] Coat, Jaecoat & Breeches £1..9..7[d]. Dictionary 6/ Buckels 4/ *July* 18, 1788.

1789.

It being the Day of the Commencement of the Constitution & Inauguration of the government. *October* 25, 1789.

1797.

A little after sunset I discovered a Winged Insect, the humming of his wings nearly resembled that of a Humbird. I noticed that in great Haste it passed from Plant to Plant, applying its hinder Part close to the Leaves, one of which I cropt & found upon it a green Egg, about the bigness of a Cabbage seed. I placed it in the House by a window. *June* 19, 1797.

Hired fifty dollars of John Roberts Jan[r] (paid) of Captain Richard Herrick twenty dollars (paid) of William Gage one hundred Dollars the same day (paid) Hired of Thomas Herrick fifty dollars (paid). *December* 11, 1797.

Sent my Son Benjamin fifteen dollars.[1] *December* 19, 1797.

[1] This entry canceled on payment of the loan.

www.ingramcontent.com/pod-product-compliance
Lightning Source LLC
Chambersburg PA
CBHW022202020726
47496CB00008B/2835